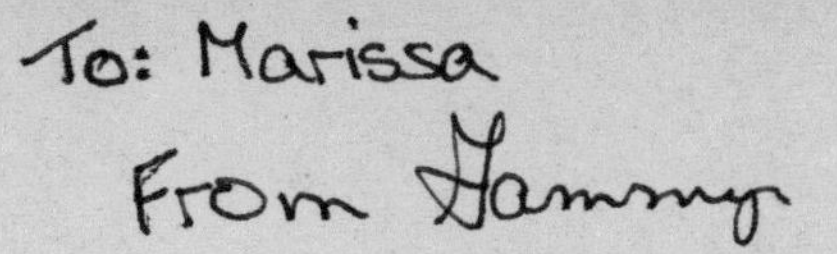

A Note from Michelle about I've Got a Secret

Hi! I'm Michelle Tanner. I'm nine years old. And I'm going to start my own newspaper!

It should be easy to find great stories. All I have to do is start in my own house! It's crammed full of people—and one of them is always doing something interesting.

There's my dad and my two older sisters, D.J. and Stephanie. But that's not all.

You see, my mom died when I was little. So my uncle Jesse moved in to help Dad take care of us. So did Joey Gladstone. He's my dad's friend from college. It's almost like having three dads. But that's still not all!

First Uncle Jesse got married to Becky Donaldson. Then they had twin boys, Nicky and Alex. The twins are four years old now. And they're so cute.

That's nine people. Our dog, Comet, makes ten. Sure it gets kind of crazy sometimes. But I wouldn't change it for anything. It's so much fun living in a full house!

FULL HOUSE™ MICHELLE novels

The Great Pet Project
The Super-Duper Sleepover Party
My Two Best Friends
Lucky, Lucky Day
The Ghost in My Closet
Ballet Surprise
Major League Trouble
My Fourth-Grade Mess
Bunk 3, Teddy and Me
My Best Friend Is a Movie Star!
The Big Turkey Escape
The Substitute Teacher
Calling All Planets
I've Got a Secret

Available from MINSTREL Books

For orders other than by individual consumers, Pocket Books grants a discount on the purchase of **10 or more** copies of single titles for special markets or premium use. For further details, please write to the Vice-President of Special Markets, Pocket Books, 1633 Broadway, New York, NY 10019-6785, 8th Floor.

For information on how individual consumers can place orders, please write to Mail Order Department, Simon & Schuster Inc., 200 Old Tappan Road, Old Tappan, NJ 07675.

FULL HOUSE™
Michelle

I've Got a Secret

Cathy East Dubowski

A Parachute Press Book

Published by POCKET BOOKS
New York London Toronto Sydney Tokyo Singapore

The sale of this book without its cover is unauthorized. If you purchased this book without a cover, you should be aware that it was reported to the publisher as "unsold and destroyed." Neither the author nor the publisher has received payment for the sale of this "stripped book."

This book is a work of fiction. Names, characters, places and incidents are products of the author's imagination or are used fictitiously. Any resemblance to actual events or locales or persons, living or dead, is entirely coincidental.

A MINSTREL PAPERBACK *Original*

A Minstrel Book published by
POCKET BOOKS, a division of Simon & Schuster Inc.
1230 Avenue of the Americas, New York, NY 10020

A PARACHUTE PRESS BOOK

Copyright © and ™ 1997 by Warner Bros.

FULL HOUSE, characters, names and all related indicia are trademarks of Warner Bros. © 1997.

All rights reserved, including the right to reproduce this book or portions thereof in any form whatsoever.
For information address Pocket Books, 1230 Avenue of the Americas, New York, NY 10020

ISBN: 0-671-00366-6

First Minstrel Books printing May 1997

10 9 8 7 6 5 4 3 2 1

A MINSTREL BOOK and colophon are registered trademarks of Simon & Schuster Inc.

Cover photo by Schultz Photography

Printed in the U.S.A.

Chapter 1

♥ Nine-year-old Michelle Tanner stared at her brand-new hot-pink notebook and sighed.

Her brain was as blank as the paper in front of her.

She twisted the end of her strawberry-blond ponytail. She scrunched up her face, trying to think hard.

She stared at the ceiling.

She stared at the floor.

She stared at the pink shoelaces in her sky-blue hightops.

Nothing!

Michelle glanced at her three friends.

"I can't think of anything!" her best friend, Cassie Wilkins, said. She gave her own ponytail a twist.

"Me neither," her other best friend, Mandy Metz, complained. She blew her bangs off her forehead.

"Don't look at me. I just came for the snacks," Lee Wagner, a friend from their fourth-grade class, said. He reached for another one of Danny's special double-fudge brownies.

"Comet? How about you?" Michelle joked. She scratched her family's golden retriever behind the ears. But Comet just thumped his tail.

"Maybe we should print the school menu," Mandy suggested. "It would fill up a lot of space."

"No way!" Michelle said. "Too boring.

Our paper has to be the best. I want every kid around to read *Kid Stuff.*"

"Yeah," Cassie agreed. "No one would want to read the cafeteria menu. It's better not to know ahead of time how they are going to torture you."

Cassie's mom made her eat a hot meal in the cafeteria every day. Cassie hated it. She thought the food was gross.

Michelle hung upside down off the end of her bed. Maybe blood rushing to her brain would help her think!

Cassie tapped her pencil against Michelle's nightstand.

Mandy doodled on her notebook.

Lee ate another brownie.

Comet fell asleep.

"I know!" Cassie suddenly exclaimed. "Maybe we could write about the thief who robbed that fancy jewelry store downtown!"

"Where did you hear about that?" Mandy asked.

"I went there with my mom yesterday. She loves to look at all the necklaces and stuff. I played with Sparkles, the store cat. You should see her. She's huge, with really fluffy gray fur. She wears a collar with jewels on it—and I think the jewels in it are real!" Cassie said.

"I heard about the robbery on the news a couple of nights ago," Lee added. "While I was waiting to hear the basketball scores."

Michelle sat up and thought a moment, then shook her head. "No, we can't print that either. You guys already know all about it. So it must be *old* news. We need *new* news. News nobody knows about till they read it in *our* paper."

"Besides, we want our paper to be just for kids," Mandy said. "We don't want to do the same stories as regular papers."

"This is hard," Lee grumbled. "Maybe we should forget about it. I feel like I'm doing homework."

"No!" Michelle insisted. "We can't give up now! My sister Stephanie works on her school paper and she says it's so cool."

"Besides, you said you wanted to save up for a mountain bike," Mandy reminded him. "We're selling the paper for seventy-five cents a copy—so we can earn a lot if we sell to most of the kids in school and around the neighborhood."

"Oh-kay." Lee sighed loudly and reached for the last brownie.

"Hey, how about sharing that?" Cassie said.

Lee licked a strip of icing off the brownie. Then he grinned at Cassie. "Sure. Want half?"

"Gross!" Cassie cried. "Eat the whole thing."

"Thanks, I will," Lee answered. He stuffed the entire brownie in his mouth.

Michelle and Mandy looked at each other and giggled. Then Cassie started to laugh too.

"Okay, so how do *real* reporters get their ideas?" Mandy finally asked.

Michelle snapped her fingers. "I know! Snoop!"

"Snoop?" Mandy repeated. She wrinkled her nose.

"You know. Like Mrs. Yoshida talked about last week in our unit on journalism. It's called 'investigative reporting.' Remember? We try to dig up news—even if people don't want us to know about it." Her eyes gleamed. "Secrets make the best news stories!"

Lee nodded thoughtfully. "It's kind of like spying, huh?"

"No wonder we can't think up ideas sitting around my room. The only news in here is that sometimes I throw my dirty clothes under the bed!"

"That's no secret," Lee teased. "Everybody in school knows that!"

Michelle threw her pillow at him.

"Okay, let's get out there and snoop—I mean investigate. There are big stories everywhere," Michelle said. "We just have to dig them up!"

Chapter 2

I don't even have to leave my house to start my snooping, Michelle thought. In her full house, there had to be someone with a secret that would make a great news story. There just had to be.

Michelle decided to start at the top of the house and work her way down. She hurried up to the top floor, where her uncle Jesse and aunt Becky lived.

Aunt Becky and Uncle Jesse were talking about whose turn it was to take their four-year-old twins, Nicky and Alex, to preschool in the morning. Boring.

Michelle crept down the stairs to her eighteen-year-old sister D.J.'s room. She heard her other sister, Stephanie, asking D.J. if she could borrow D.J.'s new strawberry-scented shampoo. Double boring!

It's okay, Michelle told herself. There's still Dad.

But Danny was on the phone with the Betty Crocker Baking Hotline. He wanted to know if he could substitute margarine for butter in one of their recipes. Super-duper boring!

Joey is my last chance, Michelle thought as she headed down the stairs to his basement apartment. Joey Gladstone was a friend of her dad's from college. He moved in with them after Michelle's mother died.

She tiptoed up to Joey's door and pressed her ear against it.

The door swung open and Michelle tumbled into the room. Joey caught her by the elbows before she hit the floor. "Thanks for dropping in," he teased.

"I . . . um . . . I just wanted to ask you for help on my *Kid Stuff* newspaper. I can't think of any good stories."

Joey started up the stairs with Michelle behind him. "I could give you some jokes. How about this: What has four wheels and flies?"

A garbage truck, Michelle thought. I heard that one in the first grade. Extra-super-duper boring!

"My family is so boring!" Michelle told her friends the next day. They huddled on the playground, talking about their snooping.

"I didn't find out one secret I could use

for our paper. But I got a great idea from Jamar Anderson on the way to school," Michelle said.

"What?" Cassie asked. She shifted her backpack to her other shoulder.

"I overheard Jamar and another kid talking about yucky stuff their dads do. Jamar's dad clips his toenails while he's watching TV!"

Lee laughed so hard, he snorted.

"That is pretty yucky," Mandy said. "But it's not really enough for a story."

"I know," Michelle answered. "But I thought we could ask everyone what their dads' most annoying habits are. That would be fun to read."

"Yeah, it would be pretty funny," Lee agreed.

"Let's do it!" Cassie said.

"I got a classified ad," Mandy said. "While I was snooping, I found out one of my neighbors is trying to sell his bike. He's going to advertise in our paper!"

"Great!" Cassie cried. "I want to write about the party Anna Abdul's having on Friday. I thought I could interview her and find out what she's got planned. Remember that treasure-hunt party she had last year? That was really cool!"

"How about you, Lee?" Michelle asked.

Lee stood up tall and puffed up his chest. "I've got big news," he bragged. "My mom is friends with Scott Larson's mom. I found out that the Larsons are moving to Ohio!"

"Wow," Mandy said. "I don't think anyone in the whole school knows that."

"That's not all," Lee told them. "I've got an amazing story idea!"

"What?" Michelle demanded.

"I'm going to find out what's inside the Mystery Room!" Lee exclaimed.

"Whoa! That's a great idea! Why didn't I think of that?" Michelle cried.

A few weeks before, a huge sparkly silver question mark had appeared on the door of an empty classroom. A sign hanging on the doorknob read MYSTERY ROOM OPENING SOON.

Every kid in school was dying to know what was inside. But the door was always locked.

If Lee could discover what was in the room, their paper would have a story everyone would want to read.

"Our first edition of *Kid Stuff* is going to be great! I can't wait until we go out and sell it on Saturday," Michelle said.

"We sold every single copy of our paper!" Michelle announced proudly. She and Cassie and Mandy and Lee plopped down at the Tanners' big kitchen table.

"It was easy too!" Michelle bragged.

"Lee took a bunch over to the baseball field—there are always a lot of kids over there on Saturdays. Mandy and Cassie handled the mall. And I went door-to-door."

"That's great, kids," Danny said. "I made you some of my California-style nachos for lunch. I thought you newshounds would be hungry."

"Thanks, Mr. Tanner," Cassie said.

"Yeah, thanks," Lee said. "I wish I could eat here every day!"

"I think your paper is a hit," Danny told them. "Kids have been calling all afternoon." He handed Michelle a list of names and numbers.

Michelle pumped her fist in the air. Mandy gave Cassie a high-five.

"All right!" Lee cried. "And we didn't even have my Mystery Room story yet. I'm going to find out what's in that room before our next paper comes out—even if I have to camp out in front of the door!"

"Call everyone back now," Mandy urged. "I can't wait to find out what they think!"

Michelle jumped up and hurried over to the phone. She grinned at her friends as she dialed the first number. But her smile disappeared almost immediately.

She hung up the phone without looking at Cassie or Mandy or Lee. Oh, no! This is awful! she thought.

"What did they say?" Lee demanded.

"I'll tell you in a minute," Michelle said. "Let me call everyone back at once." Maybe if she talked to a few more people she would have *some* good news for her friends.

Michelle dialed the next number. Then the next. Then the next.

Finally Michelle turned and faced her friends.

"What—*what?"* Cassie demanded.

"I can't believe it," Michelle wailed. "Everybody *hates* our paper!"

Chapter 3

♡ "Why?" Mandy cried.

"How could they hate it?" Lee demanded.

"Jamar's dad was really mad that we printed his annoying habit. Jamar got in big trouble. And—" Michelle began to explain.

The phone rang. Michelle felt her stomach flip-flop as she said hello.

"I hate your paper!" a girl said. She sounded as if she had been crying.

"I'm sorry," Michelle told her. "What didn't you like?"

"The story about Anna Abdul's party."

"But why?" Michelle asked. She thought Cassie's story turned out great.

"Because it said all the cool kids were invited to the party. But I *wasn't!* And I'm a lot cooler than you—or your stupid paper!" She hung up.

"Who was that?" Cassie asked.

The phone rang again before Michelle could answer. Uh-oh, Michelle thought as she picked up the receiver. I bet it's someone else who hates our paper.

"You printed my phone number in your Bike for Sale classified ad!" a woman said. She sounded annoyed.

"But how could people call you about your bike if we didn't print your number?" Michelle asked.

"Uh-oh," Mandy whispered.

"You don't understand!" the woman snapped. "It's not my ad! It's not my bike! You printed the *wrong* phone number.

Mine! I'll have to take my phone off the hook for the rest of the day!"

She hung up before Michelle could apologize. And the phone rang again.

Michelle took a deep breath and answered it.

It was Anna Abdul.

Whew! Michelle thought. Anna couldn't be mad at them. Their story about her party said only nice things.

"A lot of people are mad at me, and it's all your fault," Anna complained.

"What are you talking about?" Michelle asked.

"A bunch of kids were really upset they didn't get invited to my party. I told them my mom would let me invite only twelve kids, but they didn't care. Thanks a lot, Michelle." Anna hung up.

Michelle hung up. Instantly the phone rang. Michelle let it ring again. And again. She didn't want to answer.

"You have to get it, Michelle," Cassie finally said.

Michelle picked up the receiver. "Hello?"

"May I speak to Mr. Tanner, please?" a gruff man said.

Yes! It wasn't another angry call about the paper.

"Dad!" Michelle hollered. "It's for you." She sat back down at the table.

Danny Tanner hurried into the kitchen. "Hello? Uh-huh. Now, hold on a minute, Mr.— Oh. Oh, really? Aw, that's terrible." He looked over at Michelle with a frown. "Well, I'm terribly sorry. I'll have a talk with her. Thank you for calling, Mr. Larson. I hope your son will be all right."

Mr. Larson? Scott's dad?

Oh, no! Michelle thought. I've got a bad feeling about this!

Danny hung up and sat down at the table with Michelle and her friends. "It seems you printed a news item about the Larsons moving to Ohio."

"Everyone at school likes Scott," Michelle explained. "We thought kids would want to say good-bye. What's wrong with that?" She slapped her hand over her mouth. "Isn't it true?"

"It's true, all right," Danny explained. "Only Mr. Larson just found out about it. He and Mrs. Larson hadn't told Scott yet. They wanted to break it to him gently. Now he's really upset. Just think how he must feel! Everybody in school knew about it before *he* did."

Michelle winced. "Oh, no!" Poor Scott, she thought. He must feel rotten!

"We really messed up," Lee said.

They told Danny about all the other calls. "We hurt people's feelings and we made stupid mistakes. And there is nothing we can do about it," Michelle said.

"I don't think it's *that* bad, pumpkin.

Let's get our newspaper expert down here. I'll be right back." Danny hurried out of the kitchen.

"I should have known that the kids who weren't invited to Anna's party would be upset," Cassie moaned.

"I thought Scott already knew about moving," Lee said.

"I should have asked Jamar if it was okay to print what he said about his dad," Michelle said.

"And I should have double-checked the phone number on my classified ad," Mandy added.

Danny returned to the kitchen with Stephanie right behind him. They sat down with Michelle and her friends.

Stephanie smiled at them. "First of all, it's not great to make mistakes in a newspaper," she said. "But it's not the end of the world."

"She's right," Danny agreed. "I can't

say I'm happy about Mr. Larson's call. But even big newspapers make mistakes."

"What do they do?" Michelle asked.

"They print an apology," Stephanie explained. "They say they are sorry about the mistakes they made. Then they print the correct information. We've had to do it a couple of times on my school newspaper."

"Do you think it will work for us?" Mandy asked. "Everyone who called was really upset."

"Well, it's a start, at least," Danny said.

"Besides," Stephanie added, "most people will forget about it as soon as the next paper comes out."

"Will you help us write up our apology, Steph?" Michelle asked.

"Sure," Stephanie said with a grin. "If you promise to make my bed for a week!"

"Deal!" Michelle smiled a really big

smile. Everything is going to be okay, she thought.

"Call me when you finish your lunch, and we'll get to work," Stephanie said. She headed back upstairs, and Danny wandered into the living room.

Michelle stared at the big platter of nachos in the middle of the table. They looked delicious. But suddenly she found herself thinking about Jamar and Anna and Scott.

She stared at her friends. They stared back in silence. She could tell they were thinking about all the people they had hurt too.

"I feel horrible," Cassie said.

Then Lee took a nacho chip and munched it loudly. "Hey, I feel bad too," he told them. "But I still have to eat."

"Yeah," Michelle agreed. "Maybe everyone will forgive us when we print our apology." She picked up a chip—but froze with it halfway to her mouth.

"We've still got a problem," she said.

"What?" Mandy asked.

"A lot of kids told me they're not going to read our paper ever again. But if they don't, they won't see our apology!" Michelle explained.

"Uh-oh," Cassie said. "Now we're really in trouble."

"Not if we find a way to make sure every kid in school will want to read it," Michelle said.

"How are we going to do that?" Mandy asked.

"With *super*-exciting stories," Michelle said.

Lee groaned. "Here we go again. I already told you I'll keep working on my Mystery Room story."

"But we need more. Come on, everybody. Think!" Michelle urged. "What do all kids want to read about?"

Suddenly Michelle had it.

Teachers!

"Let's do an issue all about our teachers," Michelle suggested.

"Our teachers?" Lee exclaimed. "That's boring."

"Not just our teachers," Michelle told him. "*Secrets* about our teachers!"

Yes! Michelle thought. Every kid at school will want to read about the big secrets our teachers are keeping. And we're going to print them all in our newspaper!

Chapter 4

Michelle crouched down next to the school janitor's minivan. She could see the whole teachers' parking lot from her hiding place.

She checked her pink watch. She had about a half hour left to snoop on teachers before the bell rang.

A blue Toyota pulled into the lot.

Michelle pushed her big sunglasses higher up on her nose to hide her bright blue eyes.

She pulled her floppy denim hat

lower on her head to hide her red-blond hair.

She didn't want anyone to recognize her.

Michelle heard the car door open. She poked her head around the side of the minivan. One of the sixth-grade teachers climbed out of the car. She held a thermos in one hand and her purse in the other.

Nothing strange about her, Michelle thought. Rats! Finding out secrets was hard work.

A banged-up yellow Jeep pulled into the lot. The license plates didn't look like her dad's California plates. And it sure could use a new paint job, Michelle thought.

Ms. Iburg, the new science teacher, jumped out.

She glanced around the parking lot and then pulled out a cardboard box from the Jeep.

Then she took off her coat and draped it over the box to hide it.

Yes! Michelle thought. I smell a secret!

She pulled out her little pink reporter's notebook and a sharpened pencil.

She wrote a few notes: *Ms. I. looked around parking lot before she took box out of Jeep. Ms. I. covered box with coat.*

What could be inside that box? Michelle wondered. What is she hiding in there?

Ms. Iburg picked up the box and hugged it close to her chest. She started for the school building.

Michelle followed Ms. Iburg inside. The halls were cool and quiet this early in the morning.

Michelle walked super slow. She carefully placed each foot on the floor. She didn't want Ms. Iburg to hear her sneakers squeaking on the linoleum.

When Michelle reached Ms. Iburg's

room, she took a deep breath. Time for some serious snooping, she thought.

Ms. Iburg's door stood open a few inches. Michelle pressed her eye up to the crack. She could see Ms. Iburg standing by her desk with the big cardboard box in front of her.

Slowly, Ms. Iburg untied the string holding the box closed. She opened one flap and smiled. Her eyes almost seemed to glitter.

Michelle pressed herself closer to the door. *What does she have in there?*

Then Michelle had a horrible feeling.

Her nose started to itch. Exactly the way it did when she was about to sneeze.

She backed away from the door.

She turned to run away.

Too late. *Achoo!*

Michelle heard Ms. Iburg's heels clicking toward her. The teacher stuck her head out the door. "Good morning," Ms. Iburg called out. "I thought I heard someone out here. You're awfully early."

Michelle could feel a hot blush creeping up her neck. "H-hi," she stuttered.

The teacher stared at her through wire-rimmed glasses. "Did you need something?"

Think, Michelle, think!

Maybe she could say she was lost. Nah. Ms. Iburg might find out she had gone to Fraser Elementary ever since kindergarten.

Well, she *was* working on a news story. Maybe she should just say that.

"My name is Michelle Tanner," she said. "I'm, um, working on a newspaper called *Kid Stuff.* All the articles are for kids and written by kids. We're doing a special teachers issue. And I picked you to write about because you're new. Can I interview you sometime?"

"Sure. How about right now?"

Right now! Oh, no! Michelle thought. Me and my big mouth! I don't know what to say! What should I ask her?

Ms. Iburg led the way back into her classroom. "Just one second. I want to put this away," she said. She picked up the box and carried it over to the closet.

Michelle watched as Ms. Iburg shoved the box onto the very top shelf.

I've got to find out what's in that box, she thought. When I do, I'll know Ms. Iburg's secret—and I'll have a great story for the paper!

"Okay," Ms. Iburg said as she returned to her desk and sat down. "What questions do you have for me?"

Michelle gulped.

She sat down in front of Ms. Iburg's desk. She dug her reporter's notebook out of her backpack and flipped it open.

She stared at the blank page and tried to think. But only one question popped into her head: *What are you hiding in that box?*

Then Michelle remembered that Ms. Iburg's license plates looked different. "Where are you from?" she asked.

"North Carolina," Ms. Iburg said.

Michelle wrote the answer down as slowly as she could. She needed time to think of her next question. She could feel Ms. Iburg watching her.

"Um, what's your favorite color?" Michelle asked next. She thought it was a dumb question, but she couldn't think of a better one.

"Green. I love green," Ms. Iburg said.

Michelle needed another question—and fast. But she couldn't think of one. "I have to sharpen my pencil," she blurted out.

She slowly walked over to the sharpener, sharpened her pencil, and returned to her seat in front of Ms. Iburg's desk.

"How do you feel about homework?" Michelle asked.

Ms. Iburg laughed. "I'm for it," she said.

Hmm, Michelle thought. *No big news so far.*

What else could she ask? She stared down at the floor. She could feel herself blushing. Ms. Iburg must think I'm so lame, Michelle thought.

"Is everything okay, Michelle?" Ms. Iburg asked.

"Yes!" Michelle answered quickly. Think, think, think, she ordered herself. Got it! The perfect question!

"When did you first become interested in science?" Michelle asked.

Ms. Iburg smiled and leaned back in her chair. "I was just about your age," she said. "My grandfather decided to take me on a camping trip."

Good, Michelle thought. This sounds like a long story.

"He wanted to teach me how to fish," Ms. Iburg continued. "But I had more fun exploring the plant and animal life than I did catching fish. The only thing we came home with was poison ivy!"

Michelle laughed and scribbled down notes. The fishing story was funny. But it wasn't enough to make people buy the paper.

She had to find out what was inside that box! If she did, she would have an amazing story. And every kid in school would want to read it!

5

"Any news on the Mystery Room?" Cassie asked Lee at lunch the next day.

He shook his head. "I tried to get some answers out of the janitor. But he said I would have to wait and find out with everyone else in school."

"Guess what I found out?" Mandy whispered to the other *Kid Stuff* reporters. "Coach Mulligan likes to knit sweaters in his spare time."

Michelle gasped. "That will make a great story!"

"How did you find out?" Lee asked.

"He told me," Mandy said. "He's really proud of it. You should have heard him bragging."

"I think Ms. Iburg has a really big secret," Michelle began. "She—"

Cassie leaned across the table and put her hand over Michelle's mouth. "She's coming right toward us," Cassie whispered.

"Hi, Michelle," Ms. Iburg called as she passed their table. "I enjoyed talking to you this morning. If you have more questions, let me know."

Ms. Iburg has lunch duty today. That means her room is empty right now! Michelle thought. Perfect!

"I'll be right back!" Michelle told her friends.

"But where are you going?" Mandy asked.

"Um—I'll tell you later," Michelle said.

"And if anybody asks where I am, say I went to the bathroom!"

"Can I have your lunch?" Lee called after her.

Michelle didn't bother to answer. Lee was always trying to get her lunch. He loved the special goodies Danny packed for her.

Michelle slipped out of the cafeteria and hurried down the hall. She passed Mrs. Yoshida's room. She passed the Mystery Room with the big silver question mark on the door.

Finally, Michelle reached Ms. Iburg's room. She knew she shouldn't go inside without permission. But Mrs. Yoshida did say that some reporters would do anything to get a good story. And Michelle wanted to prove she was a good reporter.

Michelle hurried inside. She went straight to the supply closet. She opened the door and flicked on the light. The closet was long and narrow with shelves from floor to ceiling along both sides.

Michelle stared up at the box. It was all the way up on one of the top shelves. No way could she reach it.

I'll have to climb up, she thought. Carefully she put one foot on the bottom shelf. Then she put her other foot on the second shelf and pulled herself up.

Careful, she warned herself. Don't fall.

She climbed two more shelves. She grabbed the box and tugged it toward her.

One foot slipped on the metal shelf. Michelle let go of the box and grabbed the top shelves with both hands.

Her palms began to sweat.

I'm okay, Michelle thought. I just lost my balance for a second.

She stretched out her hand again—and snagged the corner of the box.

Yes!

Michelle pulled the box toward her.

She pulled open one of the box's flaps.

She pushed herself up on tiptoe so she could see inside.

Wow! Something sparkly was inside! Shiny and glittery.

Michelle had to have a closer look. Maybe if she stretched a little more she could reach inside and—

"Michelle!" someone cried. "What are you doing?"

Chapter 6

Michelle gasped!

She teetered on the shelf—and tumbled to the floor. She landed on a pile of lab coats.

Michelle shoved her strawberry-blond hair out of her eyes and saw a small, skinny kid with wild red hair peering down at her.

Great. Ronald Persley. He always blabbed to teachers. He would tell Ms. Iburg he caught her snooping.

"What are you doing in Ms. Iburg's closet?" Ronald asked.

Michelle scrambled up. She had to think fast! Her eyes landed on a shelf of supplies. "Um, Ms. Iburg said I could have some . . . construction paper."

She grabbed a few sheets off the shelf. Then she looked suspiciously at Ronald. "What are *you* doing here?"

Ronald led her over to a glass terrarium. Sand covered the bottom and a leafy branch leaned against one side.

"Ms. Iburg said I could keep my new pet in her classroom. His name is Iggy. That's short for iguana. I bought him without asking my mom, and she freaked. She won't let me keep him at home. So I came in to visit him. Isn't he neat?"

Michelle nodded. Her heartbeat slowed down. It looks like Ronald bought my story, she thought. Now, if I can just get him out of here I'll have time for one more look in that box.

"Hey, Ronald, there's a special on ice

cream sandwiches in the lunchroom," Michelle said. "Two for the price of one."

Ronald wrinkled his nose. "I don't like ice cream sandwiches."

"What about orange Popsicles? I bet you like them," Michelle said.

"Yeah," Ronald answered. "They're my favorite."

Great, Michelle thought.

"But I have to feed Iggy," Ronald said.

"I'll help," Michelle volunteered. "Is his food in here?" Michelle grabbed a white cardboard container that sat next to the tank. She yanked it open.

"Don't!" Ronald cried.

"Why not?" Michelle asked.

Too late.

A grasshopper jumped out of the container and landed on her wrist. Another one hopped out and landed on her chin.

Michelle yelped in surprise. She batted the bugs off herself.

Ronald grabbed the container away from her and closed the top. "That's why not. Look, Michelle, I don't need any help, okay? I just want to spend some time alone with Iggy."

I'm never going to get him out of here, Michelle realized. I'll have to wait to find out what is inside that box. But I will find out!

One, two, three . . . GO! Michelle darted across the street and over to the garbage cans by Principal Swanson's side gate.

She'd heard some reporters went through famous people's garbage to dig up a story. Michelle wanted to give it a try to see if she could find out any secrets about the school principal. So right after school she headed straight to his house.

I hope no one is in the backyard, Michelle thought. The side gate was too high to see over, so she couldn't check. *I'll have to risk it*, she decided.

She pulled the plastic lid off the first garbage can. *Yuck! It stinks*, Michelle thought. *Maybe there is another way to find out Principal Swanson's secrets.*

Before she could make up her mind, she heard the sound of wheels rolling over cement. Then she heard someone unlatching the side gate.

Michelle had to hide—*now!*

She dashed across the street and ducked behind a big maple tree. She pressed herself against its rough trunk.

A power lawn mower started up. Michelle peeked around the tree to see who was doing the mowing.

Hey! It was Tony Heller. Michelle didn't know the tall blond kid well. He was in fifth grade. But she knew who he was because he always won awards at school—

and because his older sister was friends with Stephanie.

Why was Tony mowing the principal's yard?

Maybe I'll wait around and find out, Michelle thought.

Tony worked hard to do a good job. After he finished mowing, he pulled the weeds in the flower bed. Then he swept the grass clippings off the sidewalk and pushed the mower into the backyard.

When he came back out, Michelle waited a minute, then strolled across the street toward him. "Hi, Tony."

Tony jerked his head up. "You scared me! I was thinking about the essay I have to write tonight."

"What are you doing here?" Michelle asked.

Tony looked nervous. "Uh—walking my dog."

"But you don't have a dog with you," Michelle said.

Tony blushed. "Right, uh—I mean, I'm *looking* for my dog. He's lost."

"I'll help you," Michelle volunteered. It would give her more time to figure out what was *really* going on.

"No, thanks. He probably found his way home on his own. Bye!" Tony ran off down the sidewalk.

Tony has definitely got a secret, Michelle thought. I think there is another good story here. And this reporter is going to find out what it is.

Chapter 7

"How is the special all-teacher edition of your paper coming along?" Danny asked Michelle that night at dinner. "Any good stories yet?"

"I'm not giving away my scoops," Michelle answered. "You'll have to wait and read the paper with everybody else."

"Way to go, Michelle," Stephanie said.

"Hey, did you hear the latest in the jewel robbery story?" Uncle Jesse asked.

Aunt Becky spooned peas onto the twins' plates. "No. What happened?"

"They think they know who did it," Jesse reported. "The police think it was the last customer in the store."

"How do they know?" Stephanie asked. "Did somebody see him?"

"Not some*body,*" Jesse said. "Some*thing.* The security camera got a picture of *her.* The video is kind of fuzzy, but they can tell it's a woman."

"What does she look like?" D.J. asked.

"Probably in her thirties," Jesse said. "With shoulder-length brown hair and wire-rimmed glasses. And she was wearing a purple and pink plaid jacket."

"Aw, I was sure the thief would have pointy ears and soft fur and a long furry tail," Joey said.

"What are you talking about?" Danny demanded.

"You know, a *cat* burglar," Joey answered.

"That is so lame," D.J. moaned.

Michelle tuned out the rest of the conversation. She had plans to make. Because she had some serious snooping to do tomorrow.

The next day Michelle got to school early—earlier than she had ever been to school before. She rushed straight to Ms. Iburg's room.

But Ms. Iburg was already there.

The teacher looked surprised. "Hi, Michelle. You're here early again. Do you need some help with something?" She smiled. "More questions for your newspaper story maybe?"

"Uh—no," Michelle said. "Actually, I was wondering if *you* needed any help . . . like, maybe cleaning the closet? I, um, wanted to do something to thank you for letting me interview you."

"The closet's fine," Ms. Iburg answered. "But I could use some help. Would you wash out these glass paint jars for me, please?"

"Sure," Michelle said. Good! she thought. The classroom sink was near the closet. Maybe Ms. Iburg would leave the room for a minute. Then Michelle could dash in the closet and take a quick peek at the mysterious box.

Michelle washed out the paint jars.

Ms. Iburg didn't leave.

Michelle washed out the paint jars again.

Ms. Iburg still didn't leave.

Ms. Iburg cleared her throat. "Are you about done with those?"

"Almost done," Michelle said. She couldn't stall anymore. She rinsed the jars and dried them with paper towels. "Anything else?"

Ms. Iburg smiled. She held up some construction paper cutouts of frogs and butterflies and other creatures. "Would you mind putting these up on the bulletin board?"

Michelle took the cutouts to the bulletin board near the closet.

"Oh, not that one," Ms. Iburg said. "The one by the classroom door."

Michelle groaned to herself. Now she was as far away from the closet as she could get!

Michelle had fun pinning up the paper frogs and other animals. Looks good, she told herself proudly when she was done.

Then she remembered the reason she was there.

The box.

How could she talk her way into the closet?

Ms. Iburg walked over to the bulletin board. "Oh, that looks great. I might have to hire you to do all my bulletin boards," she teased.

Then Ms. Iburg picked up a stack of books from a shelf by the door.

Yes! Michelle thought. She's leaving. She's going to the library. Now's my chance!

Ms. Iburg held up the books. "It's almost time for the first bell. Would you mind returning these books to the library for me on your way to class?"

Michelle held out her hands for the books. What else could she do?

♡ "And the winner of this month's Good Citizen award is—" The principal read the slip of paper and grinned. "Tony Heller!"

The audience clapped. Tony hurried up to the stage to get his award. Mr. Swanson shook his hand. He smiled and whispered something in Tony's ear.

Wait, Michelle thought as she stared at Tony and Mr. Swanson. Now I know why Tony was acting so weird yesterday. Now I know why he didn't want to talk to me.

I know Tony's secret. And I know a secret about Mr. Swanson too!

"I have a great story about this award," she whispered to Cassie and Mandy.

Cassie yawned. "What's so special about it?"

"Yeah," Mandy said. "They pick a new Good Citizen every month. Who would want to read about that?"

"But this is different," Michelle whispered. "I saw Tony mowing Mr. Swanson's lawn yesterday. And he's always winning awards. It must be because he does chores for the principal!"

"You're kidding!" Cassie said.

"That's so unfair!" Mandy said.

"You're right," Michelle agreed. "I'm going to write a story telling why Tony wins practically every award! Every kid in school will want to buy our paper!"

"Hey, Michelle, I heard about what you

said in assembly today. Is it true?" Lee plopped down across from her at the table all the way in the back of the cafeteria. "Is that why Tony wins so many awards—because he mows the principal's lawn and stuff?"

"Yes," Michelle said. "But don't tell anybody. It's one of the big stories for our paper."

"I wish I had *my* big story. I decided to try and see into the windows of the Mystery Room. But they're all covered with blue paper," Lee complained.

Cassie and Mandy joined them at the table. "Hey, there's Ms. Iburg," Cassie said. "How is your story going? Did you find out any good secrets about her yet?"

"Not yet," Michelle admitted. "Where is she?"

"Right over there by the windows," Cassie answered. "She's wearing a purple and pink jacket."

A purple and pink jacket. Why does that sound familiar? Michelle wondered.

She stared over at Ms. Iburg. There was something important about that jacket.

What is it? she thought. What *is* it?

I know! Michelle gasped. It's just like the jacket the jewel thief was wearing.

Wait a minute! The news report said the jewel thief had medium-length brown hair—just like Ms. Iburg.

And wire-rimmed glasses—just like Ms. Iburg.

And was in her thirties—just like Ms. Iburg.

Michelle thought of the glittery, sparkly things she had seen in the box in Ms. Iburg's closet. Oh, no! Now she knew what they were. Now she knew Ms. Iburg's secret.

Michelle had big news for the *Kid Stuff* readers.

Their new science teacher was a jewel thief!

Chapter 9

 *"No!"*

"Yes!"

"I can't believe it!"

"But it's true!" Michelle whispered. "Ms. Iburg is the jewel thief."

Cassie, Mandy, and Lee stared at her.

"It all makes sense." Michelle leaned across the table and counted on her fingers. "One—Ms. Iburg has a pink and purple jacket just like the thief in the video. Two—Ms. Iburg has brown hair and wire-rimmed glasses just like the thief. And three, the most important!—she's hiding a box of sparkly stuff in the closet in her classroom. I think it's the stolen jewels!"

"I can't believe it!" Cassie almost shrieked. "Oh, Michelle, that's scary! Stolen jewels—right here at school!"

"Not so loud!" Lee told her.

"Wait a minute," Mandy interrupted. "I don't get it. Why wouldn't she hide the jewels at home?"

"Because she's tricky," Michelle whispered. "Who would think of looking for stolen jewels here? In a supply closet at an elementary school?"

"Wow, that's smart," Lee said. "Really smart. No wonder the police haven't caught her."

"Do you think she's dangerous?" Cassie asked. "What do you think she would do if *she* knew *we* knew the truth."

Michelle bit her lip. She hadn't thought

of that. "I'm not sure. She seemed nice at our interview . . ."

"Maybe we should tell somebody," Mandy said nervously. "The principal, or Mrs. Yoshida."

"No!" Michelle exclaimed. "At least not yet. That would ruin our big news story."

"But, Michelle," Mandy went on. "We can't just let a thief run around loose."

"Okay," Michelle said. "Let's do this. Let's keep this a secret for now. We'll run the story on the front page. But I'll take the first two copies to Mrs. Yoshida and Mr. Swanson. Then they can call the police before she gets away."

"Great idea!" Lee exclaimed. "Then we can put out an extra edition about the arrest!" He gulped some milk. "Hey, maybe they'll even put us on one of those true-crime TV shows!"

Mrs. Yoshida came over to their table.

"Michelle? I need to speak to you for a minute."

Mrs. Yoshida led Michelle over to the cafeteria door. "The principal wants to see you in his office."

"The principal wants to see me?" Michelle gulped.

Mrs. Yoshida nodded. "Right away."

Chapter 10

Michelle felt a shiver run down her spine. She slowly walked out the door and down the hallway. She knew she should hurry. But how could she when her feet felt like lead?

At last she came to the principal's office. She went inside and gave her name to the secretary. The secretary peered at her over her glasses.

Michelle felt so guilty—and she didn't even know why!

She sat down in the outer office to wait.

Then Tony Heller came in and sat down beside her.

Michelle stared. Was Tony—the principal's pet—in trouble too?

Tony glared at her. He didn't look nervous. He looked angry.

What was going on?

"Mr. Swanson will see you now," the school secretary announced.

Michelle followed Tony into the office and sat down in front of Mr. Swanson's big wooden desk.

The principal drummed his pencil on the desktop for a moment. "Michelle, there are some rumors going around school," he began. "Rumors that Tony won Good Citizen of the Month just because he mowed my lawn. And the rumors seem to lead back to you."

Michelle blushed. So that's what this was all about! I'll get Lee for this, she thought. He promised not to tell anyone!

What should she do? Should she admit it? She was trying hard to be a good reporter. And she knew good reporters stood by their stories. That's what Mrs. Yoshida taught them.

Besides, the story was true, right? Wasn't that why Mr. Swanson was so upset?

"It's true," Michelle admitted. "I uncovered Tony's secret. I was planning to do a story on it in my newspaper. I'm sorry if the story hurts Tony's feelings. But it's not fair that he gets special treatment. The other kids should know the truth."

Mr. Swanson cleared his throat. "That's a fine speech, Michelle. But unfortunately, the 'truth' you think you discovered is not the truth at all."

"What?" Michelle shook her head. "But I saw him mowing your lawn with my own two eyes."

"You're right, he did," Mr. Swanson

said. "But he wasn't doing it to get good grades or win awards. He's trying to earn enough money to go to camp next summer. He mows—I pay. That's all there is to it."

Oh, no, Michelle thought. I really messed up.

"Besides," Mr. Swanson continued, "a panel of teachers chooses the Good Citizen of the Month, not me. Tony is a hard worker. He wins his good grades and awards fair and square.

"You see, Michelle, you jumped to conclusions without getting your facts straight. I hope you've learned how dangerous that can be."

Michelle nodded. She felt too awful to talk.

"Okay, you can go," Mr. Swanson said.

"Hey!" Tony cried. "Everyone in school is still going to think I cheated to win all my awards."

Michelle forced herself to look at him. "I'm really sorry, Tony," she said. "I'll tell everyone the truth, I promise."

"Okay," Tony said grumpily.

And I'll make Lee help me tell everyone, Michelle added to herself. That rat!

"You got me in trouble," Michelle told Lee that afternoon right after school.

Lee squirmed. "I only told Jeff Farrington."

Michelle rolled her eyes. "He tells everybody everything!"

"Well, it's lucky for you that I did tell," Lee said. "Otherwise, we would have put that story in the newspaper. Then we would be in big trouble!"

Michelle sighed. "Thanks, I think."

"Now on to our next problem," Mandy said. "What are we going to do about the Ms. Iburg story?"

"We have to be careful," Michelle said.

"We've got to be sure that it's true. We don't want to make another mistake—the way I did with Tony and the principal."

"We have proof," Mandy said. "You've got to get into that room. You've got to get to that box!"

Michelle thought a moment. Then she grinned. "I know how to get in there tomorrow morning. I've got a plan. But I need your help."

Chapter 11

Mandy's shriek echoed down the hallway.

"Help!" Cassie cried out.

"It's the only way!" Lee yelled. "We're going to have to cut it off!"

"No!" Mandy screamed.

Michelle stood near to Ms. Iburg's door the next morning and giggled at her friends. What actors!

Mandy's sleeve was stuck in the zipper of Cassie's jacket. Lee was aiming at the zipper with a pair of scissors.

Ms. Iburg rushed into the hall to see what was going on.

Everything was going according to plan.

Lee signaled Michelle to sneak into Ms. Iburg's room. She dashed into the classroom.

She headed straight for the closet. She climbed up the shelves. Hurry, she thought. Hurry, hurry, hurry!

She grabbed the box—and it crashed down on top of her.

Jewels flew everywhere. Rubies. Emeralds. Diamonds.

Then Michelle heard something terrifying.

Footsteps entering the classroom.

Ms. Iburg!

She was coming back into the room—with Mandy and Cassie and Lee!

What if Ms. Iburg caught her with all the jewels!

Quickly Michelle shut herself in the

closet. Then she began to stuff the glittering stones back into the box.

"Thank you so much!" Cassie said. She spoke *really* loud so Michelle would be sure to hear her.

"Yes," Mandy nearly hollered. "I can't believe you fixed that zipper so fast."

"Uh, maybe you should come show Mrs. Yoshida how to do that," Lee added. "She's always getting her zippers stuck."

"Yeah," Cassie said. "How about right now? She's in her room."

Ms. Iburg laughed. "I can't right now. I have to get ready for school to start. And you kids better get going too."

Michelle heard her friends leave.

Uh-oh. Now I'm stuck in the closet! If I leave, Ms. Iburg will see me. How long am I going to have to stay in here?

Then—double uh-oh—Michelle heard footsteps coming right toward her.

Michelle stuffed herself back into the

farthest corner of the closet. She spotted an old raincoat and threw it over her head.

Then she heard the doorknob on the closet turn.

What will Ms. Iburg do when she catches me?

I'm doomed!

Chapter 12

Ms. Iburg opened the closet door.

Michelle froze. She tried to breathe silently.

"What!" Ms. Iburg exclaimed. "How did this happen?"

Michelle heard Ms. Iburg picking up the jewels and putting them back in the box. Then she heard the box slide back on the shelf.

She doesn't see me! Michelle thought. Hurray!

But Ms. Iburg didn't leave the closet.

Now I'm in for it.

What is she *doing?* Michelle wondered.

Ms. Iburg walked to the end of the long, narrow closet and stopped right in front of Michelle.

Don't move, Michelle told herself. Don't even breathe. Stay still and nothing will happen.

A few moments later Ms. Iburg pulled something off the shelf next to Michelle and left. She closed the closet door behind her.

Phew. That was a close one, Michelle thought. Only one problem left. I'm still stuck in here.

She snapped her fingers. I've got it. I'll wait for the bell to ring. When the other kids come *in,* I'll sneak *out.*

Her plan worked perfectly. Cassie, Mandy, and Lee were waiting for her in the hall with worried frowns on their faces.

"Michelle!" Cassie gasped. "Are you all right!"

"What happened?" Mandy demanded.

"I had to wait for a chance to sneak out of the closet without Ms. Iburg spotting me. It was scary," Michelle admitted. "But guess what? I found out the truth!"

Michelle folded her arms. "Ms. Iburg's secret box *is* filled with jewels."

"Really?" Cassie exclaimed.

"Man, oh, man," Lee muttered.

"Yep. Now I have the proof I need," Michelle announced. "Ms. Iburg is the jewel thief. Our story runs!"

"How does this sound for the headline: Jewel Thief Discovered at Frasier Elementary?" Michelle asked.

"Perfect!" Mandy exclaimed. She and Cassie crowded behind Michelle as she worked on Danny's computer.

"Put it in extra big letters," Cassie said.

Michelle punched some buttons to make the headline big and dark. "Now, where should we put Mandy's article about the sweaters Coach Mulligan knits?" she asked.

"I think it should go in one of the bottom corners," Mandy said. "And it should be more of a boxy shape instead of a rectangle like your story. Remember how Mrs. Yoshida said that a newspaper page should be made up of different shapes?"

"Right," Michelle answered. "Give me the computer disk you typed your story on and I'll move it onto our page."

"You're getting good at this," Cassie said. "Remember how many tries it took us last time?"

"Yeah—and we don't even have Stephanie to help today," Michelle answered.

Ding-dong! Bang, bang, bang!

"That must be Lee. He's late—as usual," Cassie complained.

Ding-dong!

"I'm coming! I'm coming!" Michelle called. She hurried down the stairs, Cassie and Mandy right behind her. She pulled open the door and Lee burst in.

"I got the story! I know what's in the Mystery Room!" he exclaimed. "It's a new computer lab. I saw the janitor bringing in a bunch of Apple computer boxes."

"This is so great! Our paper is going to be amazing!" Michelle cried.

That night Michelle tried to show her family the paper. She knew they would be really proud of her for uncovering such a big story.

But everyone was busy.

D.J. was over at a friend's house studying for a big history test. Stephanie was baby-sitting. Joey was doing a show at a local comedy club. Uncle Jesse and Aunt Becky were at the movies. And her dad was working on an interview he had to do in the morning.

They will all just have to wait and read the story in the paper like everybody else, Michelle thought. *It's their fault for not being around when I have such super-amazing news.*

Finally Michelle went to bed without sharing her big news with anyone. She was almost asleep when Stephanie came in, pulled on her nightgown, and tumbled into bed.

"Hey, Stephanie," Michelle said. "Guess what?" She had to tell at least *one* person before morning.

"Wha . . . ?" Her sister sounded half asleep.

"I've got a secret," Michelle whispered across the room. "And I've got to tell somebody or I'll just pop."

Michelle waited. "Stephanie?"

"Mm-hmm?"

"You won't believe this!" Michelle exclaimed. "But I caught the jewel thief! And tomorrow morning it's going to be on the front page of my newspaper."

"That's nice. . . ." Stephanie mumbled.

"Stephanie, are you listening? I caught the jewel thief! It's Ms. Iburg, the new science teacher! I even know where she's hidden the jewels. What do you think of that?"

Zzzzzzzzzzzzzz.

Stephanie was snoring!

Michelle sighed. Stephanie hadn't heard a word. Michelle wished she had someone to talk to about tomorrow. She was excited and nervous at the same time.

She had a feeling the next issue of *Kid Stuff* would change her life—forever.

Early the next morning Michelle stood at the door to Mrs. Yoshida's room. She had two *Kid Stuff* newspapers tucked under her arm.

"Mrs. Yoshida?" Michelle said.

Her favorite teacher looked up and smiled. "Yes, Michelle?"

Michelle bit her lip. "Can you come with me to the principal's office?"

"Well, I—"

"It's very important," Michelle said. "Kind of an emergency, actually."

Mrs. Yoshida looked alarmed. She jumped up and hurried to Michelle's side. "Are you all right? Are you hurt?"

"No, I'm fine," Michelle told her. "I just want to tell you and Mr. Swanson something at the same time."

They reached the principal's office just as he was pouring a cup of coffee.

"What's all this about?" he asked. "More problems with Tony?"

"No," Michelle said. "It doesn't have anything to do with him."

Mrs. Yoshida shrugged and sat down. "Michelle says she has something important to tell us."

Michelle took a deep breath. Then she handed each of them a copy of her newspaper. "Read this."

The ticking of the wall clock filled the silent room as the two adults read.

After a moment Mrs. Yoshida's eyes grew wide.

Mr. Swanson started to laugh.

"Why are you laughing?" Michelle demanded. "We have to call the police. We don't want Ms. Iburg to escape."

"Michelle, you can't be serious," Mrs. Yoshida said. "Joan Iburg is a lovely woman. What made you think she's a thief?"

"I have proof!" Michelle insisted. "I actually saw the stolen jewels!"

Mrs. Yoshida and Mr. Swanson exchanged looks.

"Really," Michelle said. "Come on, I'll show you!"

Michelle hurried down the hallway with her teacher and the principal right behind her. She dashed through the door of Ms. Iburg's classroom and screeched to a stop.

Ms. Iburg was already there.

Michelle ducked behind Mrs. Yoshida. Suddenly she felt terrified.

"Good morning, Joan," Mr. Swanson said. "I'm sorry to bother you. But it seems we have a little problem that we need to straighten out."

He turned to Michelle. "Would you like to explain to Ms. Iburg why we're here?"

Michelle gulped. Her hands began to shake.

Mr. Swanson, Mrs. Yoshida, and Ms. Iburg stared at her.

Michelle opened her mouth, but nothing came out. Her throat felt really dry.

What would Ms. Iburg do when Michelle revealed her secret?

"Go ahead, Michelle," Mr. Swanson said.

Michelle took a deep breath. "I know about your secret."

Ms. Iburg looked puzzled. "What secret?"

Michelle clenched her hands to keep them from shaking. "I know you're the jewel thief who robbed that store downtown. I wrote an article about it for my paper."

"What?" Ms. Iburg exclaimed.

Michelle ran to the closet. "The proof is in here—on the top shelf!"

She yanked open the door and pointed.

The top shelf was empty!

The box full of stolen jewels had disappeared!

Chapter 13

♡ Ms. Iburg laughed and laughed and laughed.

Michelle's knees began to tremble. Ms. Iburg had moved the jewels. Now no one would believe her.

And worse—what would Ms. Iburg do to Michelle for blabbing her big secret to the whole world?

Ms. Iburg stood up and walked over to Michelle. She bent down until she could look Michelle straight in the eye.

Michelle thought her heart would stop beating.

"Are you looking for the box I kept on the top shelf?" Ms. Iburg asked.

Michelle couldn't speak. She just nodded her head.

"Is that what made you think I was a jewel thief?" she asked.

Michelle nodded again.

The principal shoved a hand through his thinning hair. "Joan, I—"

But Ms. Iburg shook her head. Then she reached out and grasped Michelle's ice-cold hand. "Come on," she said with a mysterious smile. "I've got a secret to show you."

Michelle looked nervously over her shoulder. But Mr. Swanson and Mrs. Yoshida were right behind her.

Ms. Iburg led them down the hall, humming to herself. They stopped in front of the door with the big question mark on it.

The Mystery Room.

Wait, Michelle thought. Lee said this is going to be a computer lab. Why are we going in here?

Ms. Iburg took out a key and unlocked the door. "Take a look," she said, and shoved the door open wide.

"Wow!" Michelle gasped. Glowing stars hung from the ceiling. Plants sat everywhere. Prisms at the windows splashed rainbows of color across the room. The counters were cluttered with microscopes and gadgets and a huge aquarium.

"What *is* this place?" Michelle exclaimed. It definitely *wasn't* a computer lab!

"It's my big secret—a hands-on science exploration lab," Ms. Iburg explained. "It's my surprise for the school. I want to show you and your classmates how much fun science can be. It's just about ready to open."

One of Ms. Iburg's eyebrows shot up. "Does anything in here look familiar, Michelle?"

Michelle studied the room—and gasped.

She ran over to the aquarium and pressed her nose against the glass.

The stones that filled the bottom sparkled like jewels. Just like the jewels Michelle had seen in the box in Ms. Iburg's closet.

Which meant . . . they weren't really jewels at all.

"You mean—they're not real?" Michelle asked.

"I wish! My car needs a new set of tires and they are going to cost me a fortune!" Ms. Iburg shook her head. "If these were real jewels, I would have cashed them in already. But they are all just glass."

Michelle was speechless. How could she have made such a huge mistake?

"Michelle, this is the second time you've jumped to a conclusion about another person. Accusing someone of being a thief is very serious," Mr. Swanson said.

Michelle felt tears sting her eyes. She felt horrible. Ms. Iburg had been so nice to her.

"I'm sorry! I was so sure this time!" Michelle blurted out. "I'm . . . I'm glad you didn't get arrested!"

Ms. Iburg laughed. "Me too." Then she sat down and pulled Michelle toward her. "I admire your curiosity, Michelle. It's a fine quality. That's what makes a good reporter. A great scientist too."

She reached for Mr. Swanson's copy of *Kid Stuff.* "You know, journalism and science have a lot in common. They're both about uncovering new ideas. But it's important in both to check and recheck our facts to prove that something is true. That's what scientific experiments are all about."

Michelle couldn't believe how cool Ms. Iburg was being. "We haven't sold any of these papers yet," Michelle told the teachers and Mr. Swanson. "I promise we'll get rid of them."

"I'd also like you to write me a two-page essay about jumping to conclusions," Mr. Swanson said.

Michelle nodded. She felt relieved. That punishment wasn't too bad.

"I'd also like Michelle to do something for me," Ms. Iburg said. "I want you to be my assistant in the Mystery Room. You'll need to come in early two days a week," Ms. Iburg told Michelle.

"That's hardly like punishment at all!" Michelle said. The Mystery Room was really cool.

Ms. Iburg smiled at her.

"I have an assignment for you too," Mrs. Yoshida said. "I want you to give our class an oral report on what can happen when a reporter doesn't check all the facts in her story."

"I can give a great report on *that* topic!" Michelle said. "No problem!"

I'll get Lee to help me, she thought. He needed to check his facts too!

"So that's why our all-teacher edition didn't come out," Michelle confessed at dinner that night.

Her dad could hardly believe all this had happened right under his nose. "I'm sorry I was busy when you tried to talk to me. Next time just tell me it is important."

"Thanks, Dad," Michelle said.

"I never want you dealing with something as serious as a jewel thief on your own," Danny said. "You have to tell me about anything that could be dangerous right away. If you aren't sure what is dangerous and what isn't—ask me."

"I will. I promise," Michelle agreed.

They finished eating and Michelle helped clear the table. Then she wandered into the living room and flipped on the TV.

"Hey, everybody!" Michelle hollered.

"Come here, quick! There's a news story on about the jewel thief. The real one!"

The Tanners rushed in and filled up the couch and chairs to watch the story.

"Police have learned that the woman in the purple and pink jacket was not the jewel thief," the newscaster reported. "Mr. Johnson, the store owner, reports that he has discovered the *real* thief. His cat, Sparkles. The jewels were stored in a gray velvet bag. The same color as Sparkles's favorite mouse toy. The jewels were found tucked beneath a counter in Sparkles's favorite corner."

The Tanner family broke up into laughter.

"Can you believe that?" Uncle Jesse crowed. "I think the lady in the pink and purple jacket should sue!"

"It really *was* a cat burglar!" Joey said.

Michelle laughed. "I'm glad to see that I'm not the only one who jumps to conclusions!"

It doesn't matter if you live around the corner...
or around the world...
If you are a fan of Mary-Kate and Ashley Olsen,
you should be a member of

MARY-KATE + ASHLEY'S FUN CLUB™

Here's what you get:
Our Funzine™
An autographed color photo
Two black & white individual photos
A full size color poster
An official **Fun Club™** membership card
A **Fun Club™** school folder
Two special **Fun Club™** surprises
A holiday card
Fun Club™ collectibles catalog
Plus a **Fun Club™** box to keep everything in

To join Mary-Kate + Ashley's Fun Club™, fill out the form below and send it along with

U.S. Residents – $17.00
Canadian Residents – $22 U.S. Funds
International Residents – $27 U.S. Funds

MARY-KATE + ASHLEY'S FUN CLUB™
859 HOLLYWOOD WAY, SUITE 275
BURBANK, CA 91505

NAME:____

ADDRESS:____

_CITY:______________________ STATE:_______ ZIP:_________

PHONE:(____) __________________ BIRTHDATE:____________

TM & © 1996 Dualstar Entertainment Group, Inc. 1242

FULL HOUSE™ Stephanie

PHONE CALL FROM A FLAMINGO	88004-7/$3.99
THE BOY-OH-BOY NEXT DOOR	88121-3/$3.99
TWIN TROUBLES	88290-2/$3.99
HIP HOP TILL YOU DROP	88291-0/$3.99
HERE COMES THE BRAND NEW ME	89858-2/$3.99
THE SECRET'S OUT	89859-0/$3.99
DADDY'S NOT-SO-LITTLE GIRL	89860-4/$3.99
P.S. FRIENDS FOREVER	89861-2/$3.99
GETTING EVEN WITH THE FLAMINGOES	52273-6/$3.99
THE DUDE OF MY DREAMS	52274-4/$3.99
BACK-TO-SCHOOL COOL	52275-2/$3.99
PICTURE ME FAMOUS	52276-0/$3.99
TWO-FOR-ONE CHRISTMAS FUN	53546-3/$3.99
THE BIG FIX-UP MIX-UP	53547-1/$3.99
TEN WAYS TO WRECK A DATE	53548-X/$3.99
WISH UPON A VCR	53549-8/$3.99
DOUBLES OR NOTHING	56841-8/$3.99
SUGAR AND SPICE ADVICE	56842-6/$3.99
NEVER TRUST A FLAMINGO	56843-4/$3.99
THE TRUTH ABOUT BOYS	00361-5/$3.99
CRAZY ABOUT THE FUTURE	00362-3/$3.99

Available from Minstrel® Books Published by Pocket Books

Simon & Schuster Mail Order Dept. BWB
200 Old Tappan Rd., Old Tappan, N.J. 07675

Please send me the books I have checked above. I am enclosing $________(please add $0.75 to cover the postage and handling for each order. Please add appropriate sales tax). Send check or money order--no cash or C.O.D.'s please. Allow up to six weeks for delivery. For purchase over $10.00 you may use VISA: card number, expiration date and customer signature must be included.

Name ____

Address ____

City ______________________________ State/Zip ________

VISA Card # ___________________________ Exp.Date ________

Signature ____

™ & © 1997 Warner Bros. All Rights Reserved.

929-19

#1:THE GREAT PET PROJECT 51905-0/$3.50
#2: THE SUPER-DUPER SLEEPOVER PARTY 51906-9/$3.50
#3: MY TWO BEST FRIENDS 52271-X/$3.99
#4: LUCKY, LUCKY DAY 52272-8/$3.50
#5: THE GHOST IN MY CLOSET 53573-0/$3.99
#6: BALLET SURPRISE 53574-9/$3.99
#7: MAJOR LEAGUE TROUBLE 53575-7/$3.50
#8: MY FOURTH-GRADE MESS 53576-5/$3.99
#9: BUNK 3, TEDDY, AND ME 56834-5/$3.99
#10: MY BEST FRIEND IS A MOVIE STAR! (Super Edition) 56835-3/$3.99
#11: THE BIG TURKEY ESCAPE 56836-1/$3.50
#12: THE SUBSTITUTE TEACHER 00364-X/$3.50
#13: CALLING ALL PLANETS 00365-8/$3.50
#14: I'VE GOT A SECRET 00366-6/$3.99

A MINSTREL® BOOK

Published by Pocket Books

Simon & Schuster Mail Order Dept. BWB
200 Old Tappan Rd., Old Tappan, N.J. 07675

Please send me the books I have checked above. I am enclosing $_________(please add $0.75 to cover the postage and handling for each order. Please add appropriate sales tax). Send check or money order--no cash or C.O.D.'s please. Allow up to six weeks for delivery. For purchase over $10.00 you may use VISA: card number, expiration date and customer signature must be included.

Name ______________________________
Address ______________________________
City ____________________ State/Zip __________
VISA Card # ____________________ Exp.Date __________
Signature ______________________________ 1033-17

™ & © 1997 Warner Bros. All Rights Reserved.